Off to the Woods

By Ellen Weiss
Illustrated by Joe Ewers

A MUPPET PRESS/GOLDEN BOOK

The big day had come at last. Kermit was
taking Robin and the other Frog Scouts on a
camping trip.

"We're all ready, Uncle Kermit!" said Robin excitedly. "We've got our sleeping bags, our tents, and everything!"

"Great," said Kermit. "Then we're off!"

It was a long ride to Misty Mountain. The
Frog Scouts sang songs all the way. At last they
arrived.

"After we set up camp," said Kermit, "you scouts can gather wood for our campfire."

Soon the Frog Scouts went off to gather firewood.

"Here's a good tree," said Marvin. "We could take some of these branches."

Everyone broke some branches off the tree.

"Maybe we should take a few more," said Mary Lou. "We want a nice big campfire."

The scouts were busy taking off more branches when Kermit appeared.

Kermit looked at the tree. "Uh-oh," he said. "I forgot to tell you one important rule of camping. Leave everything just as you find it. That includes trees. It hurts a tree if you break off its branches."

"I know," said Kermit. "Well, that's one camping lesson learned."

He went on to explain that the branches from the tree wouldn't burn well anyway. Live wood was too green and damp to burn.

Kermit picked up a stick that was lying on the ground. "This wood is dead—and dry," he said. "This is the kind of wood we should use for firewood."

"Okay, Frog Scouts!" said Robin. "Let's do it right this time."

That night the Frog Scouts made a nice big campfire—with very dry wood. After they had eaten supper, the scouts told ghost stories until bedtime.

When it was time to sleep,
they poured water on the fire
to make sure it was out.

In the morning they got ready to leave.
"We'll clean up the campsite so well," said
Marvin, "nobody will know we were here at all!"
"Wonderful!" said Kermit.

Before long the Frog Scouts were packing
the van and heading back. They sang songs all
the way home.

One month later it was time for the next
Frog Scout camping trip. Once again Kermit
drove the scouts to Misty Mountain.

After they set up camp, the scouts walked up to Kermit. "We have something to show you, Uncle Kermit," said Robin.

There, in a little clearing, Kermit saw a brand-new baby tree.

"We planted it ourselves," said Robin proudly. "Marvin's mom helped us."

"We felt awful about the other tree," added
Marvin.

"This little tree is great," said Kermit. "When
you kids grow up and have Frog Scouts of your
own, it will be very tall."

"And when we have Frog Scouts of our own," said Robin, "we'll teach them to leave everything in the forest exactly the way it is. Right, Uncle Kermit?"

"That's right," said Kermit smiling.

Here are ways you can help
keep our forests healthy:

1. When you're in the woods, gather up all your trash
   before you leave.

2. If you have a campfire, make sure you put it out
   with lots of water.

3. Leave the forest plants and flowers as they are.
   Collect interesting stones or rocks instead.